The Necromancer's Apprentice

R.M. PRIOLEAU

小力 CHIKARA PRESS

Chapter 1

— 🕊 —

MY FAMILY'S MANOR SAT IN Caristan's sparse countryside, forty miles south of the city of Lakis. The greystone was laced modestly with withering ivy, and a wooden fence marked the boundaries of the property, snaking a path among the trunks of the surrounding white birches. Some of the fence planks had reduced to rotting wood over the years.

The manor had once been a prosperous farm, producing the finest wheat and corn. Every mid-autumn, the eloquent auburn tones of the foliage around the manor painted a picturesque example of the season. The temperate winds carried the scent of fallen seeds and a promise of another prosperous harvest.

This year, the Blood Moon filled the autumn skies. Under that moon, the farmlands surrounding the manor were mostly barren, devoid of life. The once-flourishing birch forests around them had reduced to hollow, white-striped trunks with dead twigs for branches. The earth thirsted for rain; it had been months since there'd been a single drop.

Folklore and superstitions drew on the Blood Moon, which had appeared rarely over the past several centuries. It was generally perceived as a portent of misfortune, affliction, and death. I believed in neither superstition nor coincidence and rather saw the Blood Moon as a beautiful work of art. The Blood Moon, casting its copper-stained light over the drought-stricken country, brought the skies to life.

Amongst the wheat fields, I lay on my back in a bed of straw and stared up at the cloudless orange and crimson sky of dusk. A cool wind began whistling through the fragile shafts of dried wheat and brushed over my pale face.

My stomach growled, protesting the meagerness of the dinner I'd eaten earlier. I sighed and shut my eyes, attempting to ignore my body's demands for more food.

Beneath the sounds of the wind and rustling wheat, I heard footsteps approaching. I slowly opened my eyes to see my elder sister's silhouette. As she drew nearer, the trim of her long, flowing dress flitted through the soft breeze of the impending night.

"Jasmine?"

A thin smile crept upon my lips at the sound of my sister's concerned, soft-spoken voice. I sat up from my nest of straw.

Her slender, pale hands gently smoothed out the excess creases in the soft, laced fabric of her white, ruffled house dress. She gave me a pointed look. "You know that Father does not approve of your being out here alone whilst the Blood Moon has risen."

I pouted and directed my attention toward the horizon, where the crimson-touched moon had already begun peeking over the distant hills of the countryside. I shook out the excess straw that had found its way into my snow-white hair, a contrast to my sister's ebony just as my slate grey eyes contrasted with her amber ones. "It is still early, Violet," I said wistfully. "I wish Father were not so paranoid of age-old myths. He is like a child, believing in nonsense like creatures of darkness swooping down during the nights of the Blood Moon, to feast upon our souls."

Violet pursed her lips. The wind rustling through the fields sounded like footsteps approaching.

She cast a nervous glance over her shoulder toward the manor before returning her attention to me. She lowered her voice to a soft whisper. "It is not just the

Blood Moon he worries about, sister. Mother's condition has worsened."

I sighed. "Honestly, Violet, I cannot bear to see Mother's sickened condition any further." I chewed on my bottom lip and envisioned the frail, skeletal body of our comatose mother.

Violet canted her head and furrowed her brow. "But . . . you have not seen her all day."

"Something is eating away at her very soul, and it is obvious that none of us are able to help her."

Her expression fell, and tears formed, which made me realize how cold my response sounded.

I scowled. "No, Violet. Don't you *dare* cry. I hate it when you cry."

She gazed at me pleadingly, attempting hold back her tears. "I-I'm sorry, Jasmine. I'm trying to stay strong, I really am. Please . . . please go and see her for me."

Her choked words made me cringe. With a soft sigh, I reluctantly stood up. "All right . . . I will."

Smiling, Violet wiped the tears from her eyes, then extended a hand.

I took it, and we made our way back to the manor, following the narrow, shadowy path that cut through the wheat fields.

A chilly wind whisked over the part of my upper back left exposed between my hair and my dress's neckline. Was someone watching? My steps faltered, and I looked over my shoulder.

In the wheat fields behind us, shadows danced in the coppery glow of the Blood Moon above.

Chapter 2

―❧―

THE FRONT DOOR OF THE manor creaked open as Violet led me into the house. The scent of leftover dinner—boiled cabbage—still wafted through the heavy, despair-ridden air. Silver talismans, etched with the Goddess's holy symbol, and cloves of garlic adorned the doorways of each of the candlelit rooms, including my own.

I scoffed at the damnable things as I walked past my room. Father's radical superstitions were getting out of control. I hastily ripped the trinkets from my doorway and carried them to the living room, where I flung them into the hot embers of the fireplace. A pungent aroma rose from the hearth as the garlic burned, and I turned away, holding my breath.

Violet stood before me, her hands on her hips, glowering. "Jasmine, what in Celestra's name are you doing?"

Startled by her presence, I exhaled. My heart pounded. I didn't realize she had been watching. But I stiffened and held my head high as I regained my composure. "Father should keep his ridiculous trinkets away from my room."

She shook her head and stared toward the fireplace. "You could've at least spared the silver."

I followed her gaze and frowned bitterly. I saw no reason to spare something that was tainted in superstition.

"Come, Sister," she said in a calmer voice, placing a gentle hand on my shoulder.

I glanced at her hand for a moment, then looked back at her. The concern in her eyes returned, and I knew what she wanted me to do. Without saying another word, I allowed her to escort me upstairs.

After we ascended the final step, she withdrew her hand from my shoulder and strode over to one of the closed bedroom doors, from which the flicker of a brighter candlelight could be seen beneath. She knocked softly before entering the white-laced room.

I followed my sister inside and discovered Father standing at Mother's bedside, gazing over her.

"You will be all right, Lily, dear," he whispered.

His attention suddenly turned toward me and Violet. His eyes were anxious, almost fearful of our presence. Around his neck, he wore a clove of garlic, coupled with a silver charm necklace bearing the Goddess's holy symbol. Tied to his belt was a small, silver dagger, its clean blade glimmering from the flames that made the room glow.

He turned away from us and picked up a green-tinged elixir from the bedside table. He brought the edge of the vial to Mother's pale lips and slowly poured the liquid down her throat. Father then turned and walked to the desk lined with various medicines and homemade remedies, all of which had seen frequent use.

I focused on the bed, where Mother lay deathly still. Her skin was almost as white as the sheets, and her once-beautiful face was now thinned and bony. Auburn curls danced along the edges of her face as she slept peacefully. The sheets covering her body rose and fell slightly, the only indication that death had not yet consumed her.

After I'd seen enough of her, I turned back to my father.

He rubbed a small cloth along his forehead, wiping away beads of sweat. "Girls," he said, sounding exhausted, "Lily is not responding to the medicines, and I don't know how much longer she will hold on. The curse upon our family—our lands—is evident. We may be forced to leave the farm and travel north to Lakis in order to find the healer we need." He paused and turned a saddened gaze on Mother. "I must ensure that your mother will be strong enough to endure the long trip."

I blinked. "Leave the farm?" I had known this place all my life, not daring to venture beyond the birch forests.

Violet gasped. "Father! Do you realize what you are saying?"

"There *has* to be another way. . . ." I muttered.

Father looked at both of us and then sighed. "Your mother is dying. We will not find a cure by remaining here. Her life depends on us."

"We cannot risk any further harm to her body, Father," Violet protested, shaking her head. "Such a long journey will only worsen her condition."

"Do you think I am not aware of that? But it is all we can do—for her sake." Father turned to me. "I know you don't want to leave this place and all of our family's history behind, Jasmine."

I glared at him. *This won't help Mother.* "Grandpa entrusted you with this farm before he died eleven years ago. We all worked hard to maintain it like he would have wanted. Now you want to simply leave it?"

Father's gaze hardened. "Believe me, Jasmine, this decision was not easy. However, I will *not* let this damnable blight take your mother away from me."

I stood firm, crossed my arms, and held my head aloof, as though expecting him to further explain himself.

"Jasmine, don't think I'm not aware of your disapproval," he continued sharply. "This farm is all that you've known, but your mother's condition is not a normal sickness. It is a curse from the Blood Moon. We must take her to an appropriate physician in Lakis."

I opened my mouth to protest his superstitious blather, but by the stubborn look in his hazel eyes, any attempt to convince him otherwise would be futile. I held my tongue and sighed heavily.

"We will set out in two days. Travel lightly and take only what you need. I do not know when we will return." Father then dismissed us.

I was the first to leave the room. Mother was not dead; yet, somehow, the air was heavy and rank as if death itself was looming nearby. I sought solace in my small bedroom, where I gazed out the window at the Blood Moon. The midnight sky was transitioning into a deep crimson hue as the moon neared its peak.

I turned away from the window and focused my gaze on the room itself, trying to decide what to pack for the trip. I adored my books, which were lined neatly on the wooden shelf in one corner. In another corner, the door to my wardrobe was ajar, revealing the laced fabrics of some of my favorite dresses. At the foot of my bed was a large wooden trunk, and curled up atop it was my beloved feline, Periwinkle, who slept soundly.

I approached him and rubbed his onyx-colored belly, briefly rousing him from his light nap. He purred contentedly and closed his eyes again.

My family had always thought me strange for being contented by so very little. I accepted and embraced this individuality from the rest of the world. I cringed every time I saw my sister cry, something I'd never done myself.

In the end, I found peace with myself, knowing that I would never have such tears to shed. Emotions were such an impediment in life.

Chapter 3

—— ❧ ——

THE TWO DAYS THAT FOLLOWED felt like an eternity as we prepared to leave against my better judgment. Early the morning we were to leave, before the sun had a chance to rise above the birch forests, I stepped outside of the manor for perhaps the last time and felt an eerie, void feeling sweep over me and linger. We had loaded a small hay cart with Mother and what few belongings we packed. Mother lay in a nest of hay, and she was covered with a quilt. Periwinkle, who had been following me around, hopped into the cart and curled up beside Mother.

Violet tore her gaze from Mother and regarded Father, her eyes glassy. "Father," she said sharply, breaking the long session of uneasy silence, "I would like for Jasmine to keep watch over Mother while we travel. It is not often they spend time together these days, after all." With Mother unconscious, my elder sister had taken it upon herself to act in Mother's stead.

Father finished covering our packed items with a hemp tarp and looked at Violet, raising an eyebrow, then nodded slowly. Without saying a word, Father turned and went to the barn to gather the two remaining horses we owned.

Before the drought, we had kept six horses, three cows, eight goats, seven chickens, and three pigs. We had been regrettably forced to sell or slaughter most of the animals for food, but we'd been left with two horses, a mare named Daisy and a gelding named Faithful, both of which Father was adamant about keeping.

When Father was gone, I glared at Violet, frowning. "That was unnecessary."

She met my glare. "Was it? You are deliberately distancing yourself from her, and I don't like it. She is our mother, and she needs us more than ever."

"I am not 'distancing myself' from her. While I hold no objections to wanting to spend the last days with her, I do not want my memories of Mother to be tinged with the despair and suffering that currently afflict her." If she were otherwise, she would have regained strength and awoken.

Violet took a breath, as though to further argue her point, but instead fell silent, climbed in the back of the cart, and sat at Mother's side.

I boarded the cart as well and sat across from them, nestling myself comfortably in a small bed of hay and leaning my back against a portion of the tarp that covered our belongings.

For as long as I could remember, Violet had always steered clear of heavy arguments. Death was an uncomfortable feeling that Violet struggled to embrace, whereas I knew it would not be long before Mother would submit to the Eternal Sleep. It was imminent in her eyes, her body, and all our failed efforts to cure her. Those few pleasant memories from all those years ago of Mother's healthy, smiling face had been replaced by a corpse-like image of the woman I used to love and adore.

Violet pored over Mother's body. "This is a mistake," I heard her mutter.

I turned and watched Father work tirelessly to secure the two horses to the front of the cart.

The animals, whose lower ribs protruded above their bellies, stumbled as Father fought to keep them steady. I shared the same pain I saw in Father's eyes as he watched his beloved animals suffer.

When Father finished, he made one final check of the cart before grabbing the reins and standing alongside the animals. "All right. Let's be off," he called over his shoulder at us, his voice choked with pain.

We set out, and I cast a melancholy stare back at the manor, not knowing if I would ever return there again. Part of me wanted to stay in the familiar place I had known all my life, yet another part of me felt adventurous, curious of what the rest of the world had to offer.

Violet watched Father as he handled the horses and guided the hunger-weakened animals down the dirt road.

I stared at Mother in silence. She didn't wake up.

Periwinkle rose from Mother's side and padded over to me, where he curled in my lap, purring contentedly despite the heaviness in the air.

I soon found myself afraid to look away from Mother's body. The familiar scents of the farm left the air, and the cool, refreshing scent of the birch forests filled my lungs. I hesitated to look up.

Shadows overfell us, and I finally lifted my eyes. We had entered that forest of tall birch trees that I had always only seen from the manor.

The eerie white birches, seemingly devoid of life, resisted bending to the winds that whistled through their frail branches. As we traveled deeper into the dreary, uninviting place, it seemed as though the usual warm colors of autumn were practically non-existent.

The air grew colder, and the quiet sounds of the country were replaced with the occasional echoing howls of distant predators.

I looked behind us and could no longer see the entrance to the forest. The dirt road disappeared into a tree-lined portal of blackness. Looking forward, I saw more of the same, which caused me to momentarily lose my sense of direction.

I spotted many footprints in the soft dirt and realized that we were, indeed, on a well-traveled road. The treetops filtered out most of the morning sunlight, leaving the area blanketed by shadow.

The horses trudged along the road. Their combined effort had enabled them to pull the heavy cart with little difficulty thus far, though the road was far from smooth.

Violet managed to sprawl out against the back of the cart and fall asleep from the unsteady bumps in the ride.

I watched her while she slept, envious of her peaceful state. With the thoughts about Mother and feelings about leaving home swarming through my mind, I failed in my attempts to get the slightest bit of sleep. I missed my old life.

I lost track of the time while I mused. Before I knew it, we had exited the forest and were traveling a more open road, which was hilly and rocky. Off to the east, through the mesh of trees that lined the road, I could glimpse a large lake. Sunlight serenely reflected off the water.

The sunlight started waning from the dismal, grey afternoon to the vibrant, autumn hues of dusk. Most of the trees there still had their leaves, all mottled with autumn's signature colors. The atmosphere was reminiscent of our farm, though not as crisp, but nor was it tinged with death, as the manor had been.

I continued scanning the new scenery, my mind wandering over what my new life would be like, away from the home I'd known for so long.

The cart stopped abruptly, snapping my attention back to my family. Violet awoke with a start, and I heard Father's long string of curses.

Daisy had collapsed, and Faithful was on the verge of following suit. He whinnied weakly as Father examined his fallen comrade. I slowly stood up from the cart, intending to further assess the situation, but Violet grabbed my hand.

"There is nothing you can do right now, Sister," she said, shaking her head. "Please, sit down and let Father handle it."

I huffed, pulled my hand away, and reluctantly sat back down. I returned my attention to Mother, who appeared to be the same as usual. She could have died on our way to this point, and I wouldn't have known. I took Mother's cold, skeletal hand in mine and rubbed it gently with my thumb.

"There is so much death. . . ." I whispered.

Violet said nothing in reply and appeared disturbed by my words. Perhaps she was attempting to find peace within herself again. Her amber eyes quickly turned toward Father, who was still tending to the horses.

Father unhitched Daisy from the cart and spent several minutes hauling the animal's large, twitching corpse off the road as best he could. Sweat beaded his forehead, and devastation filled his eyes as he worked. Once he had finished tending to the animal, he took his place beside Faithful. He ran his hand over the animal's weary face and sighed. "We'll have to rest for a bit, but not too long," he told us, then peered into the back of the cart. "How are you both doing? Is Lily all right?"

Violet and I nodded, then looked at Mother.

"We're all right, but Mother still hasn't awoken," Violet said.

He lowered his head and said, voice shaking, "Faithful won't be able to go on much farther. At this rate, we will all be forced to walk on our own."

Violet's eyes went glassy. "But . . . but what about Mother? She cannot walk! What are we going to do?"

After a brief pause, Father raised his head to meet my sister's tear-filled gaze. "We go as far as we can, then carry her, if need be. She will survive, one way or another. I will see to that."

We all rested and shared a small amount of rations and water from our supplies. Father fed Faithful some handfuls of hay, and poured water from the waterskin into a bowl. When we consumed our meager portions, Father returned his attention to the road and resumed the journey, attempting to guide Faithful along as carefully as he could.

Leaning back, I stared up at the diminishing sunlight and listened to the quiet sounds of nature that had surrounded us. We had traveled most of the day, and I already wondered what night would bring.

The world beyond the manor didn't seem all that different. It was a frightening world, tinged with death that was somehow masked with a certain unmistakable beauty, which kept me intrigued.

Chapter 4

— ❧ —

AS THE CART SLOWLY CONTINUED along, my dry, tired gaze pored over the night-cloaked world around me.

The cart stopped abruptly again, rousing Violet and even Mother. Seeing Mother stir for the first time in weeks prompted me to instinctively lean over to her. The twitch of her head was more than enough for me to know that death had not yet taken her soul. Her face remained pale, her prominent cheekbones and thin, frail frame revealing the extent of her malnourishment.

I stroked her cold skin with shaky fingers. She neither stirred nor made a sound, but it was all I could do to assure her that she was not alone. I felt my heart pounding, but couldn't understand why. Was Death lingering over Mother? All I wanted was to see her at peace again.

Violet had her head bowed and muttered prayers to herself. Her white skin reflected the orange of the rising Blood Moon.

"Prayers will not help us, Violet," I said dispassionately. They never had before.

Violet paused in her prayers and looked at me. "Celestra will provide."

I scowled at her. "Celestra has not 'provided' for us thus far, Sister. She will not help us—no one will! Celestra has allowed us to suffer for no reason, and She will continue to do so no matter how many times you do this . . . *charade* you call 'prayer.'"

"Do *not* speak ill of the Goddess, Jasmine. She has spared us for this long. She is always with us, even when you think She is not."

"She is angry at Father."

"Father?"

"His damnable superstitions have blinded him from the truth. What god would favor such foolishness?"

Violet frowned. "You are exaggerating, Sister—"

"Am I?" I arched an eyebrow. "Have you not found it odd that we've not yet encountered any people along this road since we left home? We *still* have not found anyone to help us!"

Violet fell silent and stared down at her hands.

It had unnerved *me* that there was not a single soul in sight. Even the animals were scarce. Only the foliage retained its warm, autumn beauty.

Father returned to the cart, his face almost as pale as Mother's. "Faithful can't go any farther. He needs rest, as do the rest of us."

I looked at the weary horse, whose legs wobbled as they tried to support the animal's weight. He'd been unhitched from the cart, but he didn't seem to move. "We're resting out here? Like this?" I asked Father.

"Of course not, Jasmine," he replied. "We will find a safe place to make camp."

"What about Mother?" Violet asked.

"I will carry her," Father assured her. "Now, both of you gather what you can from the cart and follow me. And one of you get Faithful."

We said nothing more, and Violet and I climbed out of the cart, gathering the remaining supplies of food and water. Father picked up Mother's weak body and held her carefully in his arms. Violet, who carried the least, took Faithful's reins and slowly led him. The animal trudged along weakly.

Even Periwinkle seemed to realize the direness of the situation as he padded along behind me, his back arched slightly.

I trailed a modest distance away from my family, to dwell on the day's events alone. I watched the horizon, where the Blood Moon continued its ascent.

Shadows cloaked the road as late evening rapidly approached.

The shuffling sounds of my family's footsteps ahead suddenly stopped, prompting me to do the same.

"I think I see something ahead," Father said. "Looks like a cave."

I looked forward and noticed the outline of a nearby cave in the crimson-tinted light.

"Great! At least we will be hidden and safe from the elements," Violet said.

If we're not killed by whatever might be living in that cave, first, I thought.

There was a moment of silence before Father called, "Jasmine? Don't fall too far behind, dear."

Before I could answer, I heard wings flapping nearby, followed by birds squawking—several of them. How strange it was to hear them so loudly—and at night!—approaching our direction so quickly. The sound was like a hawk, but louder, so I assumed these birds were large, although perhaps many birds in unison could create such a sound.

I tensed. Even Periwinkle hissed in displeasure. I hastened to meet with Father and Violet, hoping the sound would pass; instead, it only amplified.

"What is that?" Violet murmured, looking toward the sky.

"Birds," Father said quickly. "The nocturnal, predatory ones that hunt for rodents and other small animals, I'm certain."

A hint of nervousness was in his voice, but I was unsure if it was due to uncertainty about the sounds or his concern for Mother, still draped in his arms.

Faithful whinnied weakly and shook his head. Violet gave a light tug on the reins to calm him.

"Come on. Let's hurry," Father said.

The constant flapping of wings was soon accompanied by more high-pitched squawking. It did not sound like any bird that I was familiar with.

Whatever manner of bird they were, they had apparently caught our scent, because the sounds followed us as we made our way to the cave.

The wind suddenly shifted, and I felt something swoop down near my hair. I almost screamed in surprise. Chilly air blew through my hair, and the sensation stunned me.

An eerie screech convinced me that the creatures were not ordinary birds, at all. I dared to look behind me to see if more were coming, but all I could see were the looming shadows of the forest path . . .

And my cat was nowhere to be found.

"Periwinkle?" I scanned the area around my feet.

"Jasmine!" Father sounded frantic. "Get over here, now!"

I snapped back to attention and followed the sound of his voice. I found him at the mouth of the hollow cave.

The Blood Moon's modest light was more than enough to see the distress on my father's and sister's faces.

"Father! What is going on?" I asked, and then I looked to the sky.

Before Father could answer, flapping wings and eerie shrieks came our way.

Five feathered creatures dropped from out of the crimson sky above to land before us. They were monstrous in size and grotesque in appearance, with the upper halves of their torsos resembling nude human females and the lower halves being predatory birds'. Perhaps they had once been beautiful, but their flesh had since been eaten away, decaying as if they were corpses.

"I have not seen such creatures. . . ." Violet whispered.

Faithful whinnied loudly and jerked so violently, he broke Violet's hold on the reins. He stumbled away from us in a frightened frenzy, then tripped, but before he fell to the ground, one of the creatures pounced onto him, dug its talons into his flesh, and flew up and away.

Father gasped. "Faithful!"

I watched in awe as the horse was carried off into the night sky. I couldn't imagine having that kind of strength.

A screech returned my attention to the remaining creatures that approached us, two of them focusing on me and Violet, while the other two focused on Mother and Father. A deep, purple-hued light emanated from their frightening eyes. I could only assume that these creatures were possessed by something, or perhaps their own hunger had driven them mad.

I slowly backed toward Father, not daring to turn away from the horrific creatures that watched our every move like predatory cats, about to pounce on prey.

"Violet, Jasmine," Father said, handing Mother to us. "Take your mother and hide. Now."

Both Violet and I were too stunned to argue with him. We took Mother's body—I by the shoulders, Violet by her feet—and headed for safety.

The creatures let out an ear-piercing screech and charged toward him, knocking him down and piling on top of him. The other two creatures initially focused on me and Violet were quickly drawn to the commotion surrounding Father.

Carrying Mother, Violet and I ran toward the cave, leaving the horrifying sounds of flesh tearing and Father's screams behind us.

I grimaced. "Don't look back, Violet. Now's not the time to scream, nor cry."

My warning came too late as Violet looked over her shoulder. Her steps slowed, which slowed my own. Her grip around Mother's feet loosened. She didn't scream, thankfully.

I huffed and tugged at Mother's body, attempting to get Violet's attention. We had to keep moving.

Violet finally looked back at me, tears streaming down her face, and mustered the strength to continue.

My own tears remained frozen inside me. I wasn't sure I could cry if I wanted to.

The hollow cave didn't go back too far, but some areas were shadowed enough to hide the three of us.

Still carefully holding Mother, Violet and I panted for breath.

"We cannot . . . stay here . . . for long. . . ." Violet whispered in my ear, voice shaking.

"Do you think those creatures saw us?" I asked, my gaze not leaving the mouth of the cave.

"They probably have. . . ." Her eyes went downcast. "They . . . they killed Father. . . ."

"You needn't remind me." My blood boiled with fury, while terror wrought goose bumps on my arms. The damnable emotions tried to consume me, but I remained steadfast against them.

"I saw him! And those creatures! They—!" Violet shut her eyes and began sobbing.

A small knot formed in my stomach.

"*Why*, Jasmine?" she whined.

I reached out to place my hand over hers, but slowly retracted it. "There will be time to mourn his death later, Sister. For now, we must save ourselves and Mother—like he told us to."

After her grief was spent, Violet wiped away her tears and looked at me. She nodded slowly, though her gaze remained pained.

Outside the cave, the creatures started wailing again, and soon their shadows loomed before us. One of them poked its head inside, sniffing the air, and then gave deafening shrieks as if in confirmation of our presence, vibrating the cave walls.

The creature's body was far too large to fit through the entrance, but it began chipping away at the mouth of the cave with its sharp talons.

I felt Mother stir weakly in my arms.

Violet let go of Mother. "We are trapped in this cave, Jasmine," she said somberly. "You must get out of here. I will distract them. Please, save yourself and Mother if I don't make it out alive."

My eyes widened. I couldn't carry Mother by myself. "Violet! No, you can't do this. I will not go on without you! There must be another way!"

Violet regarded me, her amber eyes gentle, and a hint of a smile spread over her face. "If it is my time to die, dearest sister, then I shall embrace it, knowing I will die protecting those that I love. However, if Celestra deems my life worthy to see another day, then I will rejoin you soon."

Even with death so near, Violet remained calm. I sighed. There was no way I could dissuade her from her choice.

Violet leaned over to kiss Mother's forehead, and then kissed my own before standing up and walking toward the entrance—and the group of ravenous creatures.

She broke into a sprint as if to pass the creatures, but they pounced on her and tore into her flesh.

Her screams were like fire burning my ears. Mother was getting heavier in my arms, but I pushed myself forward and out of the cave, hoping to get away while the creatures were preoccupied.

Mother's body was ripped from my arms. Mother was too weak to scream, but I knew what the sounds meant by now.

I desperately retreated back into the cave, where I collapsed to the rocky ground, shaking uncontrollably.

One of the creatures poked its head back into the mouth of the cave and snapped at my foot, which was dangerously close to its drooling maws. I pulled my foot out of reach, and the creature howled in frustration, causing the cave to quake once more.

I covered my ears against the noise and felt a small pebble hit my forehead from above, followed by another, larger rock.

The remaining creatures shrieked in unison once they had finished their grisly feast.

More rocks fell. A larger one landed on my midsection, causing me to gasp for air.

The ground collapsed beneath me, and I fell into a dark pit, falling, falling.

The screams of the creatures above quickly faded away. I felt the shadows of death encompass me.

Chapter 5

THE COOL, ROCKY SURFACE MY face lay against was a welcoming relief.

So, this is what it's like to be dead. I wonder if Violet is here . . . or Mother . . . or Father. . . .

I felt sharp pain and great weight on my back. All I could do was listen to the ominous howl of the wind in the distance.

The afterlife seemed so uncomfortably quiet.

I suddenly picked up the reek of rotting vegetation and old, fetid water. My eyes gradually adjusted to the darkness. I attempted to move one of my arms and heard rocks tumbling from a pile atop me.

So helpless . . . I can't stand it. . . .

I felt unable to scream for help. The more I shifted beneath the rock pile, the heavier the load became.

Another rock fell, striking me in the head and slamming my forehead against the floor, dazing me for a moment. The warm, coppery taste of my own blood bit my tongue. I closed my eyes and tried to recall all that had transpired to lead me to my current situation.

Memories filled my mind, of watching and listening to my father, my mother, and my sister being consumed alive one by one until only bones and scraps of torn flesh remained.

"Violet," I said aloud. "She escaped. She would never leave me alone."

She's dead.

My eyes burned from the tears I was unable to shed for my lost family. Ironically, I felt a certain sense of peace, knowing I would, perhaps, *never* feel the grief I perhaps should.

I sensed another presence nearby, which interrupted my thoughts. I wanted to call out to whomever or *what*ever was there, but I couldn't, not in my current state.

The musty air of the dank caverns shifted. I noticed in the corner of my eye the silhouette of a large figure swiftly moving around me. I heard a snake-like hiss moments later, and the weight of the rocks lifted off my damaged body.

I was finally freed from the rubble, and the human-like creature picked me up and hastily carried me somewhere. It emanated the same musty, putrid scent from earlier, and my curiosity arose, regarding what it was. My eyes were barely open, but it was enough to watch the darkness of the caverns transition into a natural dim light emitted by some minerals in the cave.

We entered a small cavern with several wooden cabinets and tables lining the walls. Various potions and bottles were scattered haphazardly on some of the tables. I was placed upon a cool surface, with my arms and legs spread apart and secured in shackles.

What is this? Am I being enslaved?

I managed to open my eyes fully and found myself staring up at the stalactites. I stirred, attempting to move my body once more. The noise from the shackles inadvertently drew the creature's attention, as well.

The creature's hissing grew louder as it entered the light and stood over me—an aged, human male of tall stature. Locks of ebony hair draped over the defined, skeletal features of his weathered, pale face. His long black-and-green overcoat concealed the rest of his thin frame. His dark, pupilless eyes stared at me, glowing faintly with some sort of dark aura.

After he spent a few moments studying me, his lips twisted into a satisfied smile, and he moved away.

By the time I opened my mouth to speak, he had returned again, carrying a small syringe.

"Shh. . . ." He placed a finger to his lips.

His gentle gesture eased my mind, and I relaxed. He took my hand, turning it wrist-up. Moments later, I felt a sharp pain.

The needle had pierced my wrist. I cringed as he emptied the needle's bluish contents.

Immediately afterward, I felt my strength return, my senses heighten. I looked at the stranger—my savior—in awe.

"Do not become too dependent on this," he warned in a low, raspy tone, setting the syringe on a nearby table. "Larger doses will kill you."

My gaze trailed to the empty syringe. "What was that you injected me with?"

He smirked. "It is called cyanide. Like most medicines, it cures in small doses and kills in larger ones. I have, however, been working on enhancing this formula in order to speed up its effectiveness. You are the first to be subject to this experiment."

My ignorance of pharmaceutics was doubtlessly apparent from the dumbfounded look I gave him.

I heard him chuckle under his breath.

My attention returned to the stalactites above me. "I wish we could have found you before," I murmured. "Mother was dying, and we desperately needed a healer."

"I am no healer," he replied promptly, his tone icy. "My work is kept secret from the ignorant world . . ." his gaze on me was predatory, "and it will remain so."

Is he intending to keep me here? I frowned. "Why did you save me, then? Who are you?"

He hissed in amusement. "Questions. So many questions. Normally, I would not have cared what happened to you; however, you *did* make a mess of my cave with your fallen heap of rocks. I am not the ruthless killer you think I am."

I sighed. "I've lost everything. Nothing else matters anymore."

He quirked an eyebrow. "Not even your own life?"

"You have *no idea* what has happened to me, nor do I think you even care. I'm just a . . . a 'test subject' in your eyes."

"Why, yes. Yes, you are 'just' a test subject. And, no, I do not care about your pitiful life before you decided to trespass in my territory. The past means nothing to me. But . . . the future—*that* means *every*thing."

"The future?"

He dismissively waved a hand. "Indeed. Death is a delicate and beautiful art that should be expressed in all forms. Death is *not* a . . . *convenience*." He sneered. "Moreover, you came at the ideal time for me to test my cyanide mix. Now that I know it works, I can proceed to greater things."

I stared at him, allured by his pleasant description of death, captivating and poetic.

He leaned on the edge of the table where I lay, gazing at me. "You are a young girl who is full of life—full of possibilities, full of the answers I seek."

That sounded bad. I nervously licked my dry lips and attempted to wriggle out of the shackles.

"It is not often I come across civilization, these days, since the blight upon the land," he continued, ignoring my pitiful, failed attempts at escape. "There are many things I can only do with the dead. Life, however, is unpredictable. It's challenging—and I enjoy a good challenge." He smiled at me, revealing a set of unnaturally sharp fangs.

I froze, stunned at the sight. "You're not just some old man, are you? Please, whoever—whatever—you are, just let me go. What do you want with me?"

He held up my pale, thin wrist. My pulse raced. "I saved you from premature death. You owe your life to me. The debt shall be paid back in sums of your own blood."

Perhaps Father had been right—about everything. Perhaps the beautiful Blood Moon really *was* a curse. My life had been saved, only to be taken again.

I sighed heavily. "My blood . . . I have little blood to give. The drought has been devastating."

He smirked. "It is ironic that the source of the drought is the very men who seek to destroy me."

What did he mean by that? My brow furrowed. Before I could respond, he pushed himself from the table and left the room.

He returned minutes later, carrying some folded clothes, which he set next to me. He retrieved a key from one of the many pockets in his overcoat and proceeded to unlock the shackles around my hands and feet.

For a moment, I remained in place, surprised that he had set me loose. Slowly, I shifted my body to sit upright, anticipating excruciating pain to follow, but none came. My body felt fully healed, but my mind was still reeling. *Cyanide . . .*

Maybe that was all Mother needed to get better.

"For now, you will remain my slave, apprentice, and test subject," he said, and then nodded toward the clothes. "Put those on. The ones you currently wear reek of harpy."

I unfolded the clothes: a white chemise dress, a black-laced corset, and a matching skirt trimmed with embroidered patterns. The attire also carried the scent of old blood, which made me hesitant to put the clothes on.

I looked back at him. "Do you have a fascination for women's clothing, sir?" By the time I realized how sarcastic the question sounded, it was too late to stop myself from asking.

To my surprise, he simply rumbled in laughter. "Of course not. I simply did not think my last test subject deserved to wear such lovely clothes as a corpse."

I wanted to smile. "Ah . . . y-you—You're jesting."

He maintained a steady gaze that pierced through my very soul. "Hardly, my dear."

I frowned and set the outfit down before sliding off the table. I kept my eyes on him as I backed away, not wanting to be his next victim.

He approached, and I ended up in a corner of the small room. He loomed over me as his frail hand reached out and lifted my chin up for me to meet his gaze.

"My manners elude me, dear." He smirked. "Perhaps some introductions are in order, hmm? I am Daggax'iylion. I do not expect you, a mere human, to pronounce it correctly; therefore, you will simply address me as 'Master.'" His hand gently stroked my cheek. "And you are . . . ?"

His icy-cold touch felt like death itself. I gulped. "I . . . I am . . . J-Jasmine. . . ."

"Jasmine," he repeated with a grin. "Such a lovely name for a lovely girl who will bring about the true beauty of death. I do hope you will be more cooperative than my last test subjects."

My mouth went dry. *How many times has he done this in the past?* Was my new life truly to be an expendable test subject for the crazy man's experiments? I felt as though I had died and lost everything; and yet, I had been spared by a being that embraced death.

He was a seemingly powerful creature who had somehow taken the deceiving guise of a man with a hidden agenda of his own—an agenda that I knew he would not share with me.

Chapter 6

— ❧ —

ESPITE MASTER DAGG'S INTIMIDATING DEMEANOR, he was quite the gentleman, ensuring that my needs were taken care of. Perhaps that unexpected conscientiousness was merely his way of making me gain his trust. He gave me a "room," which consisted of another small, hollowed-out cavern; a makeshift bed to sleep in, which was nothing more than a nest of hay; clothes, which were obtained from the corpses of his previous victims; and food—perhaps the only good thing that came out of the little "bargain."

My freedom was limited. I was permitted to wander the caverns of his home, but not much else. I could only imagine what horrible things he might have done, had I attempted to escape.

The dank caverns I explored snaked in many directions, a well-crafted maze that I could easily get lost in. They reeked of fetid water and rotting vegetation. The moss-covered stalactites dripped with rank liquid from whatever sat above the cave. Small puddles of greenish-brown, algae-infested water formed in spots of the cave floor. Life as I had known it had no place here.

The third day, I spent the entire afternoon trekking deeper into the twisting tunnels, hoping to find an exit not under Master Dagg's watch. As I emerged into another open cavern, the smell of rotting flesh stung my nose. My gaze turned toward the empty cages lining the walls, then trailed toward the center of the cavern, where two wooden tables sat.

The tables were covered with a jumble of unfamiliar and quite unsavory-looking instruments, tools of some sort. I approached one table, picked up a tool, and examined it. After noting its odd design—and the fresh blood that covered its sharpened edge—it dropped from my shaking hand.

Its clatter echoed through the caverns.

I jumped back, my heart pounding furiously. My gaze darted around the area, anticipating Master Dagg's entrance. I moved away from the tables and stepped in small puddles on the floor as I continued down unfamiliar paths of that dismal place.

I paused to wipe the excess liquid from my legs and looked down at the substance, which felt thicker than water.

Blood. . . .

I wiped what I could on my clothes and dashed toward the exit. A stench from above suddenly struck me, made my eyes burn. I halted, cupping my hand over my nose and mouth in a feeble attempt to suppress the reek.

Several chains hung from the ceiling, bearing . . .

I thought my eyes were deceiving me.

Is that . . . a corpse?

I examined the heap hanging above me. The carcass had rotted so much that scraps of blackened, feathery skin clung to the bones that weren't exposed. The lower torso of the unidentified creature had detached as a result of aged decomposition. Two vacant sockets stared out of what remained of the creature's face.

I stepped back, unfamiliar with and disturbed by the kind of death I saw. As I turned to leave, I heard chains rustle faintly. I looked over my shoulder, focusing particularly on the hanging corpse as paranoia arose.

Surely that thing didn't just move by itself!

I hustled for the exit, and the chains clattered more loudly. When I glanced over my shoulder again, the corpse had fallen to the ground in a heap, its body having rotted beyond the chains' ability to support it.

The corpse's blackened eye sockets had been replaced by two red-glowing balls of energy.

When it met my own gaze, the corpse let out a familiar ear-piercing shriek.

I sprinted out of the cavern as fast as I could go, my hands cupped over my ears in fear.

That sound—no, not again!

I didn't get too far before I crashed into Master Dagg, which was like hitting a stone wall. I fell backward. I stared up at him, his intense, ebony eyes intimidating.

He huffed. "What in the bloody hells is going on in the dungeon?"

Rather than wait for my reply, he shuffled off toward the larger cavern to investigate.

I silently followed and observed him at a safe distance.

Master Dagg entered the dungeon and focused on the reanimated creature on the ground, which continued writhing and screeching, though it couldn't get to its feet. He fearlessly went over and picked up the rotting thing by its tiny neck with one hand.

The creature snapped its crumbling jaws just inches away from his face.

He narrowed his eyes and let out a low, threatening growl.

It recoiled and ceased resisting.

Master Dagg examined the thing for a few more moments before looking back at me, his dark eyes focused. He brought the creature closer to me. The closer he approached, the more violent the creature became, eyeing me hungrily.

I wanted to run, but my muscles were frozen. My heart raced as I stood helplessly before him and that ravenous creature, unable to run.

With his free hand, Master Dagg grabbed my wrist and dragged me over to one of the tables. He let me go, then cleared the clutter of tools from the table with a single brush of his arm before setting the creature atop it. The clatter of the metal tools hitting the ground echoed. I winced.

Master Dagg didn't seem at all perturbed by the noise or the high-pitched screams of the creature when he opened its mouth and examined its yellowed fangs. He upturned my wrist, held it in place, and shoved the creature's head down into it until its fangs punctured the skin. The creature's jaws locked firmly into my wrist, and it began feeding upon the blood that flowed from the wound.

I screamed—not from the pain, but from the experience. I struggled but was unable to escape

Master Dagg's iron grip. My precious blood kept me alive.

He allowed the creature to feed for several moments before tearing it away from the wound and examining it again.

I felt dizzy. My eyelids fluttered.

"Yes . . . *yes!*" he rasped. "You have no idea how long it took me to test this theory!"

I focused on him and the creature again. The creature was healing rapidly. The broken, rotting flesh and skin melded together over the bone. As the face of the creature healed, it reshaped itself into the monster it had once been.

My eyes widened at the confirmation of what I'd suspected. "That . . . that thing! It's—"

"Alive?" Master Dagg smiled. "You could say that, my dear. This harpy has long since passed the realm of death and entered the realm of the undeath. It feeds on the essence of life, much like your blood. It can become invigorated just by the smell of fresh, flowing blood. Harpies are vicious creatures, you know. They will prey upon anything and everything, stripping victims down to bones in mere seconds. Moreover, they are expendable, which is why I prefer using them for many of my smaller experiments."

Harpies . . . the very things that killed my family. My face went cold. I attempted to withdraw my hand from the table, but Master Dagg kept his firm hold on me.

I glared at him. "How could you do this? These very creatures—*harpies*—killed my entire family in a matter of minutes!"

"Death is fickle in whom it takes, Jasmine," he said simply and then shifted his gaze back to the writhing harpy once more. He finally let go of my wrist and raised his hand.

Claws extended from his fingertips.

I gawked at the sight. *This has got to be a dream.*

His claws tore through the harpy's throat, severing and pulling out part of its spinal cord. My blood spilled from the creature and pooled into a small puddle at Master Dagg's feet.

Once the harpy was again reduced to a heap of bone and rotting flesh, the unnatural healing stopped, the dark magic gone.

Master Dagg placed the corpse back on the table and withdrew his hand, his "claws" also retracting.

I shook my head slowly. "You are mad. . . ."

"Those who do not understand the art of death would call me that." He smiled. "However, like all things, there is a reason for my 'madness,' Jasmine."

"Care to tell me this reason?"

He casually wiped the excess blood and gore from his hands, onto his dark overcoat. "When I'm in the mood, I might feel inclined to tell you. In the meantime, do not ask me again, or I will re-animate this creature to feast on the rest of your blood."

I gulped and nodded quickly. He sounded as if he'd enjoy fulfilling that threat, which was more than enough for me to comply with his demand.

He led me out of the dungeon, and back to a more familiar portion of the cave, his laboratory.

"It's time to eat," Master Dagg said.

I perked. Despite all of the grisly scenes I had witnessed, the thought of food immediately roused my hunger. "What are you bringing back for me this time?"

He snorted. "I am not 'bringing you back' anything. You are no longer injured and displaced, and you are more than capable of hunting your own food."

Hunt my own food? I looked at him sourly. I'd never done such a thing before, but I had always wondered how he'd managed find small fruits and vegetables like blueberries and cattails for me, despite the drought. "Have you had any trouble finding other food around here? The drought took a heavy toll on the countryside."

Master Dagg shrugged lightly. "It is not too hard to find food. Sometimes I find delicacies like eel around the swamps that lie just above this cave." He cast me a sidelong glance. "I am not particular with my food, and neither should you be."

"Oh! Of course, not!" I shook my head quickly, though the sound of eating anything from the fetid swamps was not exactly appealing, either. "I will . . . uh . . . just find some more blueberries."

He shook his head. "You will not find blueberries around here. I'd only brought some back for you before because I found some while I was out running errands. Besides, you need better sustenance, like meat."

"All right, then. What are we eating today?"

"That depends on what you catch." He flashed me a fanged smile. "As for me, I feel like eating bream tonight."

I frowned. "Do I *really* have to *catch* my own food?"

"You do, unless you wish to starve to death. Though, I *do* hope you can stomach raw seafood, because that is all these swamps have to offer—and that is the way I like it."

Before I had time to argue further, Master Dagg turned and headed toward a tunnel exit. I followed him.

Exiting the cave, I was graced with the cool, refreshing air of the outside world, a stark contrast to the rank caverns below.

The cave itself sat in the midst of swampland, which stretched beyond my line of sight. The skies were overcast, and a steady rain fell. I was barely able to see the Blood Moon through the thick clouds, but it still somehow managed to cast its crimson light upon the dreary swamp in front of us.

Master Dagg waded ankle-deep into the murky water. "Well? What are you waiting for?" he asked, smirking at me.

I arched my eyebrows. "What am I supposed to do?"

"Hunt." He gestured for me to join him in the water.

Grimacing, I slowly entered the cold water. I faintly saw small schools of fish, swimming about. I approached a cluster of fish, but they seemed to sense my presence and immediately scattered. I let out a frustrated sigh.

I suddenly heard Master Dagg's dark chuckling behind me. "You do not even know how to catch your own food," he said smugly. "You truly are a pitiful little child."

"Then show me how!" I retorted.

He turned his attention back to the water. Perhaps my eyes weren't as attuned as his, because he moved as if following something.

Master Dagg sniffed once, then stood perfectly still.

Suddenly, he snatched a handful of minnows out of the water in a movement as swift as a cat's, despite his size.

He showed me the tiny silver fish while keeping them from wriggling free from his grasp. Then he slurped them up by the mouthful.

My eyes widened in disgust. I quickly turned away and covered my mouth to suppress the nausea that came over me.

The loud sound of his lips smacking were unnerving. "That's disgusting!"

Master Dagg licked the excess fish innards from his lips and used the back of his sleeve to wipe the rest from around his mouth.

"Such a spoiled little child you are," he said, eying me icily. "But, of course, you can choose to not eat at all and continue withering away to nothing. It matters not if you are alive or dead; I will still find use for you."

I wanted to protest, but my empty belly said otherwise. With a long sigh, I turned and tried again to catch something. I stared helplessly into the swamp water, unable to spot anything. I looked back at Master Dagg, who was catching even more fish with little effort. Convinced that I would never be able to mimic his actions, I blindly grabbed into water, in hopes of catching at least one fish.

After several attempts, I acquired my first catch. It was tiny, spanning no longer than the width of my palm. The fish's wriggling tickled my hand. I grimaced.

Master Dagg laughed. "I doubt that will sate your hunger, my dear."

I writhed with humiliation inside, but kept outwardly calm. "May I cook this in the laboratory?"

His smirk faded. "My laboratory is not to be used for cooking food. You would do well to not have such . . . *particular* eating habits."

"*Particular?* I will get sick if I consume this fish raw!"

He rolled his eyes and resumed his hunt. "You humans and your ridiculous presumptions."

"Are you saying I will not get sick?"

"I am saying nothing further on the matter."

I watched him catch another handful of fresh fish and gobble them. I looked down in my hands at my own tiny catch, now dead. I wrinkled my nose. My family had always cooked even the scarce food we had. Father had once said, 'A thoroughly-cooked meal keeps the evil away.' At that point, I was inclined to agree.

I closed my eyes, slowly brought the reeking fish to my lips, and took a small bite of its scaled flesh. The slick feeling of fish scales in my mouth made me shiver. I swallowed the small piece whole, hoping the taste would quickly subside.

The meager piece eased down my throat and left an undesirable aftertaste on my tongue. My eyes burned, and I felt light-headed.

Master Dagg suddenly snatched the half-eaten fish from behind me and swallowed it whole. "The thing will spoil rotten by the time you finish eating it." He wiped his mouth with the back of his sleeve. "Perhaps later, when your hunger is more severe, you will not be so hesitant."

"I'm going to die," I muttered. "I'm going to get sick and die!"

He smirked. "The more you say that, the more it will become true."

Somehow, the thought sounded comforting. "Are these disgusting fish really your staple food?"

"Fish are more abundant, but that is not all that can be found here. There are crabs, turtles, snails, mollusks, birds, animals . . . Pretty much any living creature that treads upon my territory is fair game."

"Even humans?" I looked at him warily.

He sneered. "I do not desire human flesh, unlike others of my kind. If that were the case, you would have been in my belly by now. I, however, have found that humans make *excellent* test subjects."

I scoffed, "Could there really be *more* despicable people like you?"

He simply laughed.

Chapter 7

MONTHS PASSED. MASTER DAGG UNCEASINGLY made demands on me, molding me to the routine he wanted. At first, I resisted, still recovering from my family's untimely death. I had never known how swift death could be in the face of fear. But I recovered and came to comply grudgingly with his terms since I owed him a debt for saving my life. However, in the back of my mind, I still believed he was up to more than what he was telling me.

He'd finally granted me permission to leave the cave to hunt for food in the swamps, but that was all.

I awoke one day to the echoes of metal clashing with bone coming from Master Dagg's laboratory.

Hungry and still groggy from being roused so early in the morning, I crawled out of my sleeping spot and trudged through the caverns. On my way to the cave's exit to go hunting, I passed by the laboratory and caught a glimpse of a large, covered object on the center table. It was large enough for an average-sized human to be lying under. Curiosity arose. With Master Dagg nowhere to be seen, I was inclined to take a peek underneath the dirty cloth, but my hungry belly protested. I reluctantly acquiesced to the hunger and left the cave to hunt for breakfast.

The swamp was still dark; the morning sun had not yet risen enough to provide its modest light through the overcast sky. The air was moist and thick from the recent rains. I was gradually becoming more proficient at fishing, though I'd soon discovered the efficiency of gathering crabs and shellfish along the banks, which I preferred. The weather conditions were such that I could usually find them washed up in the mud, but that particular morning, they were scarce for some reason.

"Did Master Dagg eat all the shellfish?" I muttered. The man was a glutton; I was amazed he stayed so thin.

I was left with little choice but to fish for the remainder of my meal. I was nowhere near as good at fishing as Master Dagg was, but I managed to make a mediocre but acceptable catch before returning to the cave.

As I passed by Master Dagg's laboratory again, I discovered that whatever had been on the table before was now gone. All that remained was the dirty cloth, crumpled in a heap.

Master Dagg must have returned. I continued to my designated eating hollow, spread out my seafood catch on the small wooden table, then sat down.

The cave was pleasantly quiet while I ate, having grown accustomed to consuming raw seafood after Master Dagg's repeated scolding about "humans with weak stomachs." Father's words on cooking remained etched in my mind after I initially fell ill from my new diet, but my belly soon became strong enough to tolerate the raw seafood.

I spotted subtle movement in the shadows near the cavern's entrance and stopped eating. At first, I figured it was Master Dagg milling about with his daily tasks, but as I resumed eating, I realized the movement seemed far more erratic than Master Dagg's usual gait. I set down a half-eaten fish and stared warily into the darkness. "Who's there?"

The only response was the sound of something dragging across the cave floor in my direction.

Frowning, I stood up and inched forward to confront the strange sound. "I didn't think you were a man of practical jokes, Master Dagg," I said, narrowing my eyes at the moving shadows.

I stopped in my tracks when a foul stench hit my nose, my eyes watering from the nauseating reek of acid and rotten eggs. I cupped my hand over my mouth and nose, taking a few steps back.

A human-sized figure emerged from the shadows and limped slowly in my direction. The thing suddenly let out a low, guttural growl, convincing me it wasn't human.

I stood in shock, my heart pounding through my chest.

The creature limped faster and reached me with unnatural speed before I could get away. Its breath was foul. It grabbed my bare arm, its touch icy cold, and tugged at me.

I screamed, but my voice echoed to no reply.

I was truly alone.

I struggled to resist the overpowering creature, a humanoid abomination covered in rotting flesh. Within its empty eye sockets were two, familiar glowing orbs of dark magic. The creature growled furiously, attempting to pin me to the ground.

I screamed again, fighting against the abomination's firm grip, but soon fatigue brought me down, and it overpowered me. I fell on my stomach. The creature pressed me down on the cave's cold ground. It wasn't long before my body slumped down in fatigue. Lying on my stomach, my face pressed to the cave's cold ground, I felt my consciousness drifting.

A sharp pain on the back of my neck roused me. The creature had latched its fangs onto my bare skin. It began feeding hungrily upon my blood.

When the creature's sickening saliva came in contact with my skin, I felt a hot, burning sensation. The rest of my body went numb, and I could no longer move my limbs. Tears froze in my stinging eyes. I felt helpless, unable to even scream as the creature continued draining what little blood I had.

My eyes grew heavy, and darkness pressed toward me.

I shut my eyes, then felt the weight lift from my body and heard snarling nearby. My eyelids fluttered open slightly, enough to gaze upon the silhouette of another, larger figure.

The abomination was being single-handedly restrained by the newcomer, who hissed in annoyance.

I turned my head, resting my cheek upon the cold cave floor, and glanced up at the sound. My rescuer stepped into the dim light of the cave, and I recognized Master Dagg. The pupils of his eerily glowing eyes were slitted like a feline's.

I shut my eyes again. *This is not happening.* I attempted to shake the uneasiness from my mind.

I reopened my eyes and witnessed the abomination gnawing at Master Dagg's hand, in a futile attempt to break free of his grip.

The acidic saliva that drooled from the creature's mouth burned through a portion of Master Dagg's leather overcoat sleeve before contacting the bare skin of his arm. Instead of eating at his flesh, the acid dissolved, leaving him unscathed.

In retaliation, Master Dagg clawed through the creature's frail neck, splattering the blood it had stolen from me. He withdrew his crimson-covered hand, and the blood ran down his fingers to the sharpened points on the ends before dripping down into small puddles on the ground. He tossed the remnants of the creature to the ground before approaching me. He leaned over to examine the back of my neck and ran his bloody, clawed fingers across the wound.

His chilling yet concerned touch made me grimace. He picked me up and carried me off to his laboratory, where he continued his examination.

He pored over me for several minutes. After what sounded like curses in a language I was unfamiliar with, Master Dagg hustled over to one of the shelves.

I wasn't sure what was happening, but he seemed nervous. I lay on my back in silence, staring toward the stalactites above, expecting him to have some experiment in store for me.

Moments later, Master Dagg reentered my line of sight, carrying a vial in one hand and a syringe in the other. Both items contained equal amounts of a colorless liquid that looked like water, except it was thicker. He placed the edge of the glass vial to my lips and poured the tasteless contents in my mouth. He set the vial down and gently massaged my throat, encouraging me to swallow.

After I ingested the liquid, Master Dagg injected the syringe's contents into my wrist.

For a moment, I felt my paralysis subside, then my innards felt as though they'd been set on fire. I writhed, my vision blurring, then clearing—blurring, then clearing. I caught a glimpse of Master Dagg observing me before I felt him placing his hand over the wound on the back of my neck.

He loomed over me, uttering something incoherent, and a strange crimson glow emanated from his arm.

The magic felt hot against my skin. The paralysis returned, coupled with complete blindness.

Unlike before, however, I was able to scream. "S-stop! Stop it, you madman!"

Master Dagg didn't acknowledge me and continued with his strange experiment.

Minutes later, the paralysis subsided again. I could barely twitch my toes, but it was more than enough to assure me that the reversed effects of my condition were permanent. When my vision cleared enough, I focused on Master Dagg's dark eyes, confused. *What has he done?*

He finally pulled his hand away from my neck, the glow leaving his arm. "You are lucky I returned when I did, Jasmine. It seems my undead experiment caught the scent of your warm blood and decided to have a snack." He sighed, shaking his head. "Such a shame, really. It took me quite a while to find such an ideal ghastly creature for my newest experiment."

I gawked at him, my strength somehow renewed. Slowly, I sat up from the examining table and stared off at the rest of the laboratory. I felt the back of my neck for the wound, but it was gone. It no longer hurt, either.

"Am . . . am I dead?" I asked in a whisper, my eyes widening.

Master Dagg chuckled. "No, but you would have been, if the creature's contagion in your body had spread any further. Fortunately, the formaldehyde mixture you ingested, coupled with the ricin I injected in your bloodstream, was enough to make your body emulate the properties of an undead, thus making you immune to the contagion. While your body remained in that state, I was able to draw upon enough energy to heal that wound on your neck."

His words all sounded like gibberish to me. "What disease? What did you do to me?"

He snorted. "I saved your damned life; however, something tells me that was a mistake."

"You are a madman! You and your crazed *experiments*!"

Glowering at me, he grabbed me by the neck. I gagged, and he squeezed my windpipe, leaving me gasping for air.

"I will remind you that I am *still* your master." His voice no longer even sounded human. "You *will* learn to address me as such, or I will reanimate that creature and allow it to feed upon your live body until you are nothing more than skeletal remains."

Death didn't seem terribly bad; the promised preceding torment, however, disturbed me.

Master Dagg slowly released my neck.

I caught my breath. Rubbing the painful imprints his fingers had left in my skin, I scowled and spat, "Yes . . . *Master*."

* * *

Another month went by. The life I'd once known had become nothing more than a faded memory. Master Dagg instilled fear in me, reminding me of my place and demonstrating his dark powers. He threatened me on several occasions to make me one of his undead thralls, should I ever defy him.

Most of the time, however, his moods were erratic.

I had a dream one night that I lived in a faraway land, with people I didn't know. I woke up startled. The dream had felt too real to be just a normal dream. Was that my family?

"Family? What family?" Master Dagg asked, when I inquired him about the dream.

"Do you not know what 'family' is?" I quirked an eyebrow.

He snorted. "Do not belittle me, girl."

"Then tell me the truth." I paused, and then added, "Please."

"You speak of the past. I live for the future. Perhaps, at some point in your pitiful life, you had a family, but no more. Now, do not ask me about such trivial matters again."

"Yes, Master."

* * *

Master Dagg's peculiar ways never ceased to amaze me. He was a master of the dead—an *arcanist*, as he preferred to call himself. His craft was not widely accepted, so he had gone into isolation in the dank caves, where he could practice his dark arts in peace.

After many horrific close encounters with creatures of the dead and undead, it wasn't long before my own interest in the arcanic arts grew. Fortunately, Master

Dagg was pleased and willing to teach me. We both shared a certain love for knowledge of life and death.

I came to regret the day I called him a madman. He was, in fact, a beautiful artist and a master of his trade.

And my old life was sacrificed so I could be his beloved test subject, his *apprentice.*

"Do not fear death; embrace it," he always told me.

My love for the Art came without resistance or hindrance. I endured every experiment he performed, every spell he cast, and every substance I was injected with, fully aware of the risks. I could not think of a better place to die than with my beloved master, doing what he had loved.

Enduring his experiments did not come without a price, however. I felt the effects of the spells and chemicals after each session, sensing a part of my own soul dissolved. The void in my heart continued to grow, further disrupting my faint emotions.

Despite the consequences, I adored him. He was more than just my master—he was the entity that soothed the darkness plaguing me inside. He unlocked emotions in me that I thought I never had—sadness, happiness, regret—and fed upon them in his own search for what he called, "the Greater Knowledge."

"What is the Greater Knowledge?" I asked him one night, as we worked in the laboratory.

He smiled faintly and stared off into the distance. *"The Greater Knowledge . . .* It is defying all that is perceived as truth and becoming one that is incomprehensible. It is *being* the contradiction in a world of conformity."

I furrowed my brow, unable to respond to his riddling words.

"The human mind cannot comprehend the actions of the omnipotent." He smirked. "Many have tried. All have failed."

"The actions of the omnipotent? Like the gods?"

"If that is what you wish to believe."

Trying to understand him was making my head start to hurt. "Why can't you just give me a straight answer?"

He stiffened, his eyes glowering at me. "I've already told you once, girl: Do not badger me again with your trifling questions. Now, go fetch me more blood samples from the dungeon." He pointed toward the laboratory's exit.

I hung my head and replied sourly, "Yes, Master."

Chapter 8

—❧—

MASTER DAGG HAD BEGUN TEACHING me how to properly preserve his collection of poisons and spell components. I assumed he would eventually have me keep his beloved laboratory maintained while he was out running his daily errands.

Master Dagg was an excellent teacher, but he almost always overwhelmed me with more information than I could retain in one night.

"Repetitiveness is what trains the mind," he once told me.

I foolishly argued back in a mocking tone, "Repetitiveness is what makes the mind turn to mush."

He slapped me once across the mouth, and my bottom lip started to bleed. "Do not try my patience, girl."

I sucked the blood from my painful, bleeding lip and lowered my head, remaining silent.

I couldn't argue that his words eventually held true after he put me through weeks—months—of repetitive and monotonous lessons. While not a full-fledged arcanist like Master Dagg, I became confident enough in my own skills and knowledge of the Art to do small tasks on my own.

The lessons never stopped coming, and Master Dagg's absence became more frequent during the day. There were many times I was tempted to question him about his daily whereabouts, but I knew better.

One morning, I awoke late, still sluggish after another long, tedious night in the laboratory. I crawled from my sleeping spot and dragged myself through the quiet caverns. Master Dagg had evidently left me alone again—as he quite often did, after my many months of enduring his lengthy lectures and tedious assignments. I didn't know if it was simple trust that inclined him to risk that much—no doubt he was well aware of the possibility that I might use his beloved laboratory without his permission—or if there was another reason for his errands.

In any event, the thought of using his laboratory without him was tempting, but obviously a trap. I knew better than to dabble in things I didn't fully understand.

I peered out the cave entrance at the dreary swamps. The looming clouds shrouded the misty wetlands in a blanket of grey shadows.

I went out to catch my breakfast. I'd been glad the day Master Dagg allowed me to leave the cave at will, even though I was not allowed to tread beyond the swamps.

It was ironic that someone who specialized in the art of death and undeath cherished this small pocket of wetland.

The aquatic life was abundant this morning, much to my relief. "Thank the gods he didn't touch the shellfish this time," I muttered.

After filling my belly with a hearty breakfast, I wandered the swamp, meditating on the peaceful, invigorating sounds. The place possessed a beauty of its own, and it was so far away from civilization that it was unlikely anyone would find him there.

Or so I thought.

My quiet meditation was interrupted by the sound of footsteps sloshing through the murky waters. I initially thought it was Master Dagg, but the noise sounded too slow, too hesitant, as if the intruder was unsure of their destination. I spotted the silhouette of a large figure a modest distance away, with the build and walk of a human male.

I gasped. "Is he . . . really *alive*?"

I couldn't recall the last time I had seen another living being, other than Master Dagg and the swamp life. Master Dagg never had visitors—and he certainly would've not been very pleased to find one there while he was still away. I licked my dry lips, pondering what to do.

"Miss!" Concern filled the man's regal-sounding voice. "What are you doing out here in these treacherous lands?"

I narrowed my eyes at the stranger. Something about him unnerved me. "N-no. I . . . I must be seeing things. You are not really here. This is all my imagination."

"Stay right there! I'm coming!" The man trudged through the shallow waters.

When he finally stood before me, I stared down at his steel-plated boots. *Perhaps I am not delirious, after all.* But what was he doing here? I remained silent, keeping my face hidden with my snow-white hair.

"Are you all right, miss?" he asked softly. He waited a few moments before gently placing his gauntleted hand on my shoulder.

My body tensed from his steel-cold touch. I slowly turned my gaze up to realize he wore magnificent armor branded with Lakis's city emblem. His emerald eyes reflected a mix of concern and curiosity.

"Miss? Are you hurt? Can you understand my words?" he asked, peering at me.

I glanced in the general direction of the cave, fearing Master Dagg's sudden return. I wanted to run, but doing so would've risked the stranger discovering Master Dagg's hidden home.

Turning back to him, I sighed. "I am fine. Please, leave."

His thin, jet-black eyebrows raised, and he slowly lifted his hand from my shoulder. "Leave you? In these swamps? You must be mad. You are lucky you haven't been eaten by that accursed creature."

I glowered. "What manner of creature do you speak of?"

He glanced around the swamps before returning his attention to me and lowering his voice. "It is a Dragon."

My eyes widened. *A Dragon? Here in the swamps?*

"A terrible black Dragon with the face of a skull— and he is the very cause of this dreaded blight that our beloved country has been forced to endure for many months."

"Surely, you jest." I gave a small smile, amused. "Dragons are such rare and elusive creatures. I have not heard such news. I assure you, sir, there are no

Dragons here—only fish." I gestured to the small schools of minnows that swam around his ankles.

He glanced down at the fish, then regarded me again with a hint of a smile. "Allow me to make your acquaintance, miss. I am Banin Solanum, leader of the Hemlock Hunters of Lakis. We've been tracking down a certain Shadow Dragon necromancer for several months, now. Alas, our travels finally led here into these swampy lands. The Dragon is responsible for the deaths of many men, women, and children. His necromantic arts are the very source of this never-ending affliction on our country. Undead and other anomalies have been spotted around here on a daily basis since the Dragon took up residence a few months before the blight began."

I stared through Banin, speechless. I recalled Master Dagg's mention of men who hunted him. *No . . . it can't be.*

"Please, believe me when I tell you that your life is in danger the longer you remain out here. He holds no remorse for the living and only seeks to use the Forbidden Arts to make these lands suffer for his own twisted amusement."

I shook my head slowly. "No . . . I will not leave." I backed away from him. *I can't let this man discover Master Dagg's laboratory.*

Banin watched me for a moment, then extended both hands out to me in a calm and reassuring gesture.

"Please, don't run, miss. I am only here to help you. I will take you back to Lakis where you will have access to food, medical attention, and accommodations. Will you at least tell me your name?"

"No," I took another step back. "I will not. Go away! Leave this place and never return!"

As he advanced, I turned and sprinted farther into the wetlands—and in the opposite direction from Master Dagg's home.

For a few minutes, he gave chase, calling out to me. Soon, however, he slowed to a halt, probably fatigued from his heavy armor.

I glanced over my shoulder, ran deeper into the wetlands, and hid behind a tree. I peered out from behind the wide trunk toward Banin's lonely figure in the distance. Moments later, he turned and left the swamps. I waited a while longer to ensure he was gone for good before emerging from my hiding spot and hustling straight for the cave, not looking back.

I went to the laboratory, where I sought something—*anything*—to keep me busy. I retrieved one of the notebooks from the table, pulled up a chair, and began reading a random page.

Master Dagg returned shortly after, carrying two bags full of supplies.

Glancing up from the notebook, I noticed the stern yet quick scrutiny Master Dagg gave me. My heart pounded. I knew that look—he saw right through me.

Strangely, however, rather than inquire about the day's events, Master Dagg kept silent and began unloading one of the supply bags.

Tension built as I resumed my "reading." The silence was deafening. After a few minutes, I slumped further down my chair, hiding my face behind the notebook.

Suddenly, I heard his raspy breathing close to my ear.

I yelped, heart pounding. I glanced up to find him standing behind my chair, peering over my shoulder.

"You have been staring at that same page since I returned," he said. "Is such a simple illustration of an oak leaf too advanced for your little human mind to comprehend?"

I shuddered. The question sounded rhetorical, but he appeared to be waiting for me to answer.

Finally, I shut the notebook and lowered my head. How would he react to Banin's visit? "You had a visitor today. While I was out hunting, a man came with the intent to take me away and find and kill a Dragon of sorts for its many heinous crimes. I did not lead him to the cave, but he treaded dangerously close." I looked at him nervously.

"Banin." Master Dagg let out an annoyed growl. "I know all about him. He and his band of idiots intend to kill me for a crime I am not responsible for. I am an arcanist—"

"You are a *necromancer*."

I felt a sharp pain in my cheek.

"Do not correct me again, you foolish girl," he said, "or I will sever that tongue of yours."

I shivered and rubbed my red, stinging cheek, dropping my gaze. "F-forgive me, Master Dagg. I did not mean it as an insult. It's just that you work with the dead on a daily basis. You are a master of the art of death. That is what a necromancer is, yes?"

"'Necromancy' is a term coined by those who do not understand nor appreciate the true beauty of the Art. You would do well to remember that, Jasmine, else I will find other, more creative ways of reminding you."

I cringed. "That . . . that will not be necessary."

He pulled away from me and resumed unloading his other supply bag, his demeanor abruptly changing. "Good, because I would *hate* to have to destroy a perfectly good test subject due to insolence. It has been almost a year since I rescued you from your impending doom." He paused and looked at me. "Do not make me regret my decision."

I slowly shook my head. "Of course not, Master."

Another moment of silence swept over the laboratory while Master Dagg rearranged some covered jars on one of the shelves.

I swallowed, eventually mustering the courage to look at him again. "Master Dagg, may I ask you something?"

"Yes?"

"Are you the cause of this death-inducing blight?"

Master Dagg simply gave me a sharp-fanged smile, making him appear more frightening than comforting. "Is that what he told you? That I am some evil creature who is responsible for this blight? Is that what your feeble little mind has been manipulated to believe?"

"It's what I was told about you." *I have nothing else to judge you from since you've chosen to keep your private life private from me,* I wanted to add.

He scoffed, "And you would rather believe the lies of a stranger than the words from your Master? You truly are an ignorant little girl."

I pursed my lips. "There is one thing you've never told me: Are you really a Dragon?"

The smile returned to his face, and he regarded me with mild amusement. "Do you think I am?"

"Banin spoke of a black Dragon that resides in the swamps. I don't want to 'think' you are that Dragon or not. I want to know the facts."

"Do you, now? Interesting. You certainly did not feel this way moments ago when you were so quick to believe what you wanted and take it as fact."

I sighed and threw my hands up in frustration at his sharp tongue and sharper mind. "All right, I'm sorry,

Master Dagg. I wish to know the truth about you. I wish to know why Banin is hunting a Dragon. I wish to know the source of this blight."

"More questions." He laughed and turned to place another covered jar on the shelf with the others. "Banin is a vile man, bent on ignorance. His hatred for me is derived from mere assumptions and misunderstandings. He's become more of a thorn in my side than anything else. Like most slayers, he believes the Dragons are the bane of existence and the cause of the world's sufferings. He would love nothing more than to be rid of our kind, once and for all. While I'm not a religious man, even I know that it is against the Goddess Celestra's will to harm our race in any manner. I practice necromancy, or the Forbidden Arts—as ignorant humans more elegantly call it—for my own knowledge and understanding. I have no intentions or desires to abuse what I consider a 'hauntingly beautiful' art."

I furrowed my brow in confusion. "So . . . *you* are really the Dragon he is hunting?"

"Indeed I am." Once he had finished rearranging his supplies, he traversed the laboratory, gathering stray books.

I frowned, watching him. "You say you are the Dragon, yet you appear to be human. . . ." As he passed by, I handed him the notebook I'd been "reading."

He snatched it from me and smiled shrewdly. "Our kind possesses the ability to shape-shift into other forms at will." After gathering the rest of the books, he went to the bookshelf and began arranging them one by one. "You ask many questions which you already know the answers to," he continued, his back to me while he worked. "Yet you fail to ask the most obvious one."

I paused, considered his words, and asked, "What do you hope to understand from working with the dead?"

"Despite my physical appearance, I am very old, Jasmine. When a Dragon dies, they pass through what is called the Twilight, a stage in which their body returns to their creator, the Goddess, Celestra. There is still so much in this world I have yet to experience, and I wish to preserve my life just a little longer. It is believed that life preservation is something that only the gods themselves are capable of, but my studies of the dead and undead have opened up new discoveries contrary to this notion." His smile widened. "I feel as though I am so close to perfecting this. Now that you have come, it is all but a matter of time."

"Are you trying to become a god, yourself?"

He chuckled darkly. "No, my dear, though . . . it would be nice, wouldn't it?"

"Then, are you simply trying to live longer than most Dragons?" I canted my head.

He approached me and leaned against the edge of the table, looking thoughtful. "I care not about what the other Dragons do. My issues are my own. That is my prerogative."

The notion of having such god-like abilities disturbed me. *What would become of the world should someone like Master Dagg acquire such power?*

"Now that you know my secret, I guess I will have to kill you, hmm?" he joked, though I could hear slight seriousness in his tone.

"N-no, you don't need to do that. I will not tell anyone of this, I swear."

"Good." His smile faded, and his gaze hardened. "Banin did not see you come in here, did he?"

"No! Of course, not!" I said promptly. "However, I think he knows you reside somewhere in the swamps."

Another annoyed hiss escaped his lips. He picked up a stray beaker containing dark blue fluid and examined it. "There is one thing I truly hate about slayers: They are persistent. If he wants to deal with a necromancer, then I will send forth an army of zombified harpies for his pleasure." He covered the beaker and stored it securely on the top shelf. He headed for the exit and stopped in the laboratory's entryway. "I've a new task for you. First, separate three units of vampiric blood into those small vials there." He gestured toward one of the tables, where a jumble of empty vials and tubes were scattered.

"Afterward, heat the vials, then add two drops of coriander extract to each of them and wait until the blood curdles. Extract it into one of the glass jars on the shelf. Do be certain all of this is completed before I return."

I glanced at the vials and then back to him, nodding slowly. I had watched him do that tedious task many times before. Certain types of vampiric blood turned acidic when heated and could easily eat away at whatever it came in contact with, if a person wasn't careful.

"Master Dagg, may I ask you one last thing?"

He gave another annoyed sigh as he turned back around. "Yes? What is it?"

"What is the true cause of the blight upon our lands?"

He crossed his arms. "The cause of the 'blight' is the gods' choosing. There is no evil monster and no wicked, wild magic causing this. It is the natural life cycle of the world. It has been happening since the dawn of civilization and will continue to happen in the future. The world suffers, only to recover once more. That is how the balance between life and death is maintained. Feebleminded lesser creatures will believe just about anything due to fear. They fear what they do not understand. That is why Banin and all the other wretched Dragon slayers in the world are foolish, believing in such ridiculous notions and superstitions. Soon, however, they will learn from their mistakes."

"Is it . . . *natural* to be amongst the only forms of life out here in the swamps? Is it *natural* to not encounter anyone or anything else from the outside world for so long?"

"The swamps are not a place that most humans would care to visit on a regular basis. My reason for being here is to get away from life so that I can focus on death." He paused.

I frowned, no less confused than before.

He scoffed, "Believe what you will, Jasmine. Your mind is fragile and naïve like the rest of them. I speak from centuries of experience. If the words of this old Dragon mean so little to you, then I will not waste my breath trying to convince you, otherwise."

Before I could reply, he stormed out of the laboratory in a huff, leaving me to continue my work in silence.

If Master Dagg came here to escape life, then am I truly alive?

Chapter 9

— ❧ —

ONCE I HAD FINISHED MY task, hunger struck me again. Master Dagg was still away, and I decided to go hunting again.

The cave was quiet, save for the faint, pattering sounds of the rain above and the stray winds that passed through small crevices in the caverns. I went to my sleeping chamber to change my clothes. The long black-trimmed and frilled white dress had begun showing signs of tearing in different spots. I could only imagine how beautiful the dress must have looked when new, worn by Master Dagg's previous victim. I felt strange, tainted, wrapping myself in the clothing of someone who had probably been so much purer than I was and who had once been full of life and energy. I changed into a cleaner, knee-length black dress of a similar design. I never understood why Master Dagg spoiled me with such beautiful gifts.

After getting dressed, I left the cave and surveyed the dark, dreary wetlands, draped in shadows. Rain poured down and caused a mist to fog the air. Neither rain nor mist showed signs of relenting. Large puddles had formed near the banks, soon to merge with the larger bodies of water. For a moment, I simply stood and allowed the rain to drench me. Strands of my snow-white hair stuck to the sides of my face and along the back of my neck. My wet dress clung to my skin.

I endured the chill that ran through my drenched body in order to savor the cool, refreshing air. The skies, though cloudy, were dark enough for me to determine that it was nearing dusk, an optimum time for hunting. After much practice, I had learned the times of day when the larger morsels of food would emerge.

I proceeded toward the banks and waded into the shallow waters, in search of food. With the constant pouring rain, I knew it wouldn't be long before the water rose even higher. The raindrops made it difficult to spot the fish below the water's surface.

After several minutes of searching, I spied a medium-sized carp swimming near the bank. As I moved in to catch it, I noticed a large shadow moving across the ground. I stopped and looked toward the skies.

The large creature circling the area was practically camouflaged against the dark clouds, leaving only a faint outline in the sky. It held its pattern for several minutes, as if watching me from above.

I remained perfectly still and kept my eyes on it, preparing to sprint for the cave entrance should the creature attempt to dive toward me. *What is it?*

Through the sound of the rain, I picked up the sound of metal clanging nearby.

I glanced away from what circled above, toward the new sounds, and through the mist, I spied a cluster of men in the distance. I hesitated, fearing that I had already been spotted. Rather than sprint for the cave, I began treading deeper into the swamp. The water level continued drawing further up my legs.

The band of eight men drew nearer. They were all dressed similarly, with various types of weapons drawn. Banin led the group.

I hastened my steps, sloshing noisily through the water.

"Miss!" Banin's voice boomed.

I froze and looked behind me.

"What are you doing out here?" Banin yelled over the rain. "It's dangerous! Please, come back before you get hurt!" He turned and motioned to the rest of the group. "Hold! Sheathe your weapons, men!"

The other men stopped and complied with their leader's request. Banin gestured to one man, who dashed toward me.

I immediately broke into a sprint to get away from the stranger, intending to run as far away from the cave as possible. Glancing behind me, I saw the armored man still giving chase—and his long strides meant he was approaching quickly.

I changed my course to a zigzag to hopefully slow him down. As I switched directions, my left foot suddenly sank, and the rest of me kept moving forward, causing my foot to torque unnaturally and sending pain down my leg.

I tumbled to the mud in a heap, whimpering in pain. Rain blurred my vision.

The armor-clad man caught up to me, pulled me effortlessly out of the muddy mess, and then carried me back to his comrades.

I tried to resist, but my body was still recovering from the shock of the ankle injury. I stared up at the sky, hoping to find that mysterious flying creature again, but it was gone.

I felt my body slip gently out of the stranger's arms and into Banin's own.

"Girl, are you mad?" he said, glowering at me. "There is a Dragon afoot, and you are foolishly running around these swamps!"

I stared coldly into Banin's eyes, trying to hide my fear. Master Dagg still hadn't returned from his errands, and I didn't want to see his displeasure if he ever caught me in Banin's clutches.

Banin tore his gaze from mine and observed the surrounding the wetlands. He held me close to his body and yelled out to the shadows dancing about the area, "We know you are here, necromancer! You were foolish enough to show yourself in Lakis with that pathetic disguise. You cannot fool us any longer! Show yourself!"

I doubted Master Dagg would show up, but I still watched the area expectantly.

As the rain finally began showing the slightest sign of calming, the creature in the skies returned, circling above us, its shadow looming like a hungry vulture.

Several large, feathered corpses fell from the creature and into the murk around us. Banin and his men scrambled about to dodge them.

The corpses littered the surrounding swamp, and Banin's face paled. "Have you become such a feeble old Dragon that you can no longer withstand my blade? Are you truly so weak and pathetic that you toss corpses at us, now?"

We all stared at the skies in silence, only to realize that the real trouble came from below. Even in Banin's arms, I could feel the vibrations coming from the swamp. Water parted, seeping into newly formed crevices all around us.

From the murky water emerged decomposing harpies, covered in mud and filth.

The harpies moved like marionettes, as puppets to a master's will. Their eyes had been replaced with crimson orbs of magic.

The foul creatures encircled us. In unison, they gave a horrific, resounding shriek that pierced my ears and brought on memories I tried to forget.

At Banin's command, his men moved to attack. His own grip was solid, holding me protectively to his armored chest while the battle ensued. Somehow, I felt more uncomfortable being in Banin's arms than I did knowing that we had been surrounded by an overwhelming number of zombified harpies.

The armored men made quick work of the monsters, severing heads and spilling blackened blood until there was nothing left but heaps of feathers and bone. The last one fell, leaving the swamps once again quiet, save for the sound of the steady rain.

The creature above us ceased circling, and it gracefully swept down and landed before us.

The creature—a beautiful and majestic Dragon— had mottled scales that ranged from dark green to obsidian. The membrane around its wings was old and frayed in several places. Two large horns protruded from the Dragon's skull-like head and curved around its jaw lines. Perhaps the Dragon had once possessed a face, but if it had, the flesh had long since decayed.

Attached around its neck was a small, glass phylactery, which pulsated with a strange yet familiar dark magic. The Dragon's ebony eyes regarded us with a cold stare as sickly green acid drooled from its maws. It cloaked its torn wings about its body and lowered itself to the ground, as if ready to pounce on us all.

I saw something familiar in the Dragon's eyes.

My gaze widened, and I whispered, "Master . . . Master Dagg?"

A small chuckle rumbled from Banin. He glanced at me, then shifted his attention back to the Dragon. "So, you have some feeling toward this girl, do you?"

Master Dagg hissed, glared at me, then acknowledged Banin. "If you would rather have the girl than me, then take her and leave this place. Never return, or you will face something far more horrid than undead harpies."

Banin raised his eyebrows.

I looked away, feeling so used and helpless at this point. "No, Master Dagg. I . . . I don't want to go back with Banin. I would rather die here."

Banin dropped me in the mud. Before I could react, he drew his longsword from its sheath and aimed it at my face. "Perhaps he has tainted you, girl," he said, voice low. "You may not even be a living being. Prove to me that you are not another undead creature, and I will spare your life."

Panicked, I looked back at Master Dagg, expecting him to save me. The old Dragon remained in his spot, watching the scene as if amused.

I nervously looked back at Banin. "H-how am I supposed to do that? Must you open me up and see my beating heart for yourself, to be convinced that I am not undead?"

Banin cast a brief glance at Master Dagg before studying me again. I could see hesitation in his eyes as he lowered the blade to my chest. "Perhaps."

"Wait!" I huffed and held out my wrist. "Feel my beating heart. See for yourself that I am alive."

He paused and looked at my tiny, pale wrist. He took off one of his gauntlets and felt my quickened pulse, then huffed and promptly released my wrist.

"Does this girl truly mean nothing to you, Dragon?" He put his gauntlet back on and looked up to Master Dagg, exasperated.

Master Dagg curled himself up comfortably on the ground, appearing unintimidated by the Hemlock Hunters' presence. "If it means being rid of you imbeciles once and for all, then, yes, she is as worthless as a piece of lint."

Banin laughed, shoved me aside, and approached Master Dagg. A few of the other men grabbed my arms, leaving me able to only watch helplessly.

"You are not as strong as you used to be, necromancer." Banin pointed his longsword at the Dragon's throat.

Master Dagg snorted, apparently unfazed by the cold steel aimed at his scales. He flicked his forked tongue out, as if eager for Banin to follow through with his blade.

Banin's hand never faltered even as his blade struck Master Dagg's neck, drawing blood.

The Dragon gave a small grunt. He slumped weakly, causing the blade to drive in deeper.

"*No!*" Eyes wide, I tried to stand, struggling against the men's restraint, but they kept me on my knees.

Banin withdrew his sword from Master Dagg's neck and swiftly thrust the blade into the Dragon's heart.

I swallowed, feeling sick to my stomach. *He did not even bother to fight back. Was this what he wanted all along?*

After giving the Dragon's body a series of stabs and slices through his vital organs, Banin shook his sword a few times, then retrieved a cloth from a pouch at his belt and wiped off the excess before sheathing the weapon.

He stood back and studied Master Dagg's corpse before turning his attention back to me. "That was . . . *too* easy," he said uncertainly.

I spat. "No. He would rather die than deal with the likes of you—and I would, as well."

Banin laughed, approached me and lifted my chin to make my eyes gaze into his. "Are you daft, girl? He's a necromancer. He's probably already found a way to turn himself into an undead creature. It's strange, though. I haven't known any Dragon to *not* put up a fight. Tell me what you know about him. What are his plans?"

I kept silent.

"Why do you insist on defending that vile creature?" Banin grabbed both of my arms. "Do you really want me to kill you for being in affiliation with a necromancer?"

I glared at him.

He sneered. "No, on second thought, I think killing you would be far too easy. Tell me why you hold that Dragon in such high regard? What has he told you?"

Banin's questions continued, but I remained uncooperative. Master Dagg had taught me the value of patience. *Now I truly understand the annoyance Master Dagg has for Dragon slayers.*

"Bah! Enough of this!" Banin finally released me.

I rubbed my arms, sore from his grip, and warily stared at him a moment before turning my attention to Master Dagg, who lay in a bloody heap. I'd never seen him like that before.

I limped past the Hemlock Hunters and fell to my knees beside the Dragon's body. I carefully ran my hand over the multiple bleeding wounds. There was so much blood I buried my face into his scaly side, my eyes burning. I longed to cry, but no tears came.

One moment, I thought I felt the faintest breath of air come from Master Dagg, and I examined him closely. Either the old Dragon was truly dead, or he was feigning it well.

"Get away from him, girl," Banin said, drawing nearer. "His body will be taken to Lakis."

Over my shoulder, I glared at Banin. "Haven't you done enough? You've killed him, now go away!"

"He will not be dead if you become his new vessel."

"You will have to kill me before I let you and the rest of your vile men take him."

Banin smirked. "So be it."

I stared as the Hemlock Hunters drew their weapons and approached me and Master Dagg. I was prepared to die with my master—or, perhaps, I was already dead.

Nothing else mattered anymore.

Chapter 10

M Y GLARE REMAINED LOCKED WITH Banin's gaze as I slowly pulled away from Master Dagg's body and stood up. The pain in my foot was excruciating, but I somehow felt myself able to endure it.

"Approach with caution, men," Banin muttered to his comrades. "The Dragon's dark magic might have already taken hold of her."

As the men closed in on me, I heard nothing but the rain dancing across the swamp. I saw nothing but the dark shadows surrounding me.

Then the steel blades glinted at me, briefly reflecting my pale features. Whatever beauty I had once possessed was forever lost. All that remained was an empty shell of a young girl, free from life, forever enslaved to death.

And these men had killed my master.

My feet edged toward the man whom I'd learned to despise as much as Master Dagg did. *This has to be a dream—no, a nightmare.* I couldn't fight the men even if I wanted to. They overwhelmed me in numbers and strength. Slowly, I extended my hand toward the blurred, shadowed image of the Hemlock Hunter's face, hoping the man before me was but an illusion. Perhaps I had finally stepped over the threshold of death and viewed the world as it truly was.

How long would it take them to send my body to death, as well?

I felt Banin grab my hand. He used my weight to fling me to the murky ground in submission, and I found myself staring up toward the cloudy sky.

His hand came close to my face and lifted one of my eyelids up to examine me closely. While my eyes burned terribly from the stinging raindrops, the remainder of my body kept still. When would they kill me?

Banin exhaled and released me, as if he had seen enough. "It's starting."

What is starting?

The air suddenly cooled. Chills ran along my spine, and I shivered uncontrollably. I felt as if my body were being controlled.

Loss of blood? Loss of my soul? Loss of my sanity? My mind swirled with a deep desire to kill Banin, frightening me. I yearned to see his blood spill and hear his death rattle. I wanted to scream at him, but all that came from my lips was a hiss that terrified me.

Banin turned me over and pointed the tip of his longsword at the back of my neck. The sting of the ice-cold steel against my skin sent another chill through my body.

"It is too late to save the girl. He has already tainted her, it seems. We must hurry before the disease spreads further."

Disease? Is that what he calls it now? I scowled. "You are a vile creature, bent on hatred. Go ahead and slaughter me like the pig you think I am! Death is far more preferable to a life of suffering under the likes of you!"

After a small pause, I felt the blade puncture the skin on the back of my neck.

"So be it—"

A loud thump interrupted him, followed by the screams of his men.

My breathing faltered as I looked up with weak, tired eyes, instinctively seeking Master Dagg's body.

But he was gone.

The old Dragon's massive form had disappeared, leaving only a small imprint behind in the mud.

I suddenly detected the reek of acid and burning flesh. One by one, each of the armored men fell to their knees, holding their burning faces.

Banin was the last one standing, while his comrades writhed around him. He caught my gaze and gave me a swift kick in the ribs with his steel boots.

I gasped in pain, feeling bones crack upon impact, and I was too weak to scream. My eyelids fluttered, and my vision blurred as he kicked me again. A wave of sharp pain erupted from my rib, and I gasped for air.

"Is that all you can do, you feeble old Dragon?" Banin yelled, sounding panicked. "Attack from the shadows? You are nothing but a coward—a coward, a criminal, and a murderer of thousands of innocent lives, thanks to you and the dark magic you have blighted this country with! You *will* face me, Dragon! You will face me, or I will continue to make this pitiful girl suffer!"

He kicked me a third time, shattering more bones and causing the entire left side of my body to go numb. The bitter taste of my own blood stung the tip of my tongue.

The Dragon suddenly landed over me, spreading its four legs wide as if to protect my body.

My blurred vision could barely make out Master Dagg's grey underbelly, which rippled with a well-defined musculature. Though I couldn't see his face, I somehow knew he was watching me.

I heard the Dragon's rumbling voice. "I told you to take her and leave this place." His voice was heavier than before, full of malice.

"She cannot be saved," Banin retorted. "You have sickened her with the same dark taint you possess. It is time I destroy the source of the problem—*permanently*."

Master Dagg stiffened defensively. "That was all I needed to hear uttered from your wicked tongue, Banin."

The scales of his underbelly brushed against my face. He was low enough to protect me from incoming blows, but not so low as to crush my small, feeble body. I felt the muscles near his front legs jerk, as if he were clawing at the armored warrior.

I wanted to watch the battle, but Master Dagg's body obstructed my view.

I finally heard the first screams of pain from Banin and cringed. The sound was followed by claws ripping through steel and flesh.

Master Dagg roared, lifted himself off me, and pinned Banin's broken body to the ground with one of his claws. I turned my head and caught a glimpse of the aftermath.

Injured, weaponless, and helpless, Banin stared up at the Dragon with terrified but determined eyes.

Master Dagg appeared rather amused. "I could kill you. In fact, I feel very inclined to do so, but I will not.

I can think of a far better punishment for the likes of you."

Banin opened his mouth to speak, but no sound came. His eyes rolled back in his head, and his eyelids fluttered closed. Blood slowly oozed out from under his body, tinting the swamp's greenish-brown waters a dark crimson.

Master Dagg picked up the unconscious Hemlock Hunter in his claws and carried him back to the cave.

I attempted to drag myself back to my feet but fell backward in the shallow water. The back of my head hit against a protruding rock, and I couldn't pull myself up.

My head throbbed, and my eyes grew heavy as I stared up at the overcast sky above.

I entered the realm of darkness, unsure when I would ever awaken.

Chapter 11

—— ❧ ——

DARKNESS ENCOMPASSED ME FOR WHAT seemed like hours. It was beautiful in its own right, peaceful, yet lonely.

The darkness soon turned to swirling, hazy grey, and I wandered there for a time. Part of me wanted to remain and escape whatever pains awaited me in the land of the living.

The silence was suddenly broken by two voices from the sky. The voices reverberated throughout the area, sounding distant yet familiar.

"To suffer is to learn the pains of another," said one, old and oh-so-amused.

"No! What are you doing? Stop!" That one was younger, almost desperate.

"You never knew what it meant to suffer. You never truly felt pity for those people."

"You know nothing of my past, Dragon! Release me this instant!"

I stopped my endless trek and turned my eyes up toward the void above me. Banin's terrified screams rang through my mind and made my head throb. I quickly covered my ears to drown out the noise.

I felt a sharp pain in my heart, and my body shuddered. Looking down at my chest, I saw spots of blood seeping through the tattered remains of my once-elegant dress.

Banin's cries echoed again.

* * *

I slowly awoke from the void to the sights and sounds of Master Dagg's laboratory. *How or why am I here?*

As I gazed up at the stalactites, I realized I lay outstretched on one of the examining tables, my limbs secured in shackles. Banin lay beside me, limp and still.

The man had been stripped almost nude, with only the simple undergarments covering his lower essentials remaining. Blood covered his chest, which was ridden with numerous black tattoos. A portion of his chest, over his heart, was stitched closed.

Master Dagg walked by, noticed me, and gave me a faint smile. He was human again, but he appeared frailer than before. His skin was sickly and colorless; I thought he was going to simply fall over dead at any moment.

"Just in time, my dear," he said gently, stroking my cheek. "It is done."

I stayed silent and stared at him, confused.

He held his hand over a part of my chest. I looked down and noticed there were stitches there, too. "Your broken ribs punctured your heart. I tried to repair it, but . . . your heart is very sensitive to my touch. Half of your heart lost its function and rotted away, but I managed to bring life back into it. Part of my blood is transfused into you and links to the phylactery you now wear." He picked up a mysterious glass charm that hung from a cord around my neck. "The power of the phylactery will assist the other half of your heart so that it may function as normally as possible."

I felt as if I was awakening from another terrible nightmare. The glass phylactery swirled with a mysterious blue magic that glowed faintly, pulsating in time with my own heartbeat.

"Have I . . . *died*?" I whispered.

Master Dagg smiled. "Not quite, Jasmine. However, you have come dangerously close. Part of you has died, but I reanimated it through arcanic means. Essentially, you have managed to step among life, death, and the undeath—and you have allowed me to achieve my greatest goal."

His smile faded, and his eyes looked very tired. After releasing me from the shackles, he leaned weakly against Banin's table.

I sat up slowly, wincing from the pain of the stitches in my chest. I still felt weak even as the new blood began pumping through my veins.

Banin stirred, and I realized that he wasn't dead after all. It took him a few moments to realize where he was before he rested terrified eyes on Master Dagg. "Why . . . why am I still here? What did you do to me?"

"I have made you suffer," Master Dagg said weakly, voice rasping. "I have made you become your worst enemy. I have made you embrace your own fears and ignorance. I have given you life again."

Banin gasped. "*What?*"

"Your heart was so blackened with hatred and ignorance that I had no choice but to remove it. I have given you mine, instead."

Banin gasped and struggled against the restraints, frantic and enraged. "N-no. *No!* I will *not* believe your lies!"

Master Dagg watched him until he exhausted himself and stopped struggling, then proceeded to remove the restraints. "Then don't. You will soon learn the truth."

When Banin was freed, he simply lay there, staring up at the stalactites in disbelief. "W-why did you do *this*?" His voice quivered as though he was going to cry. "Why did you turn me into one of your . . . *experiments*?"

"You are hardly an 'experiment,' Banin. For all the years you've spread lies and tormented me, you will soon know the very same. See the world through my eyes. Feel the pains I've felt. Learn to understand me and my kind as you've failed to do so in your past life."

Master Dagg pushed himself from the table and watched the Hemlock Hunter expectantly. When the man didn't budge, he said, "Are you going to deny your own freedom, Banin?"

Banin shrank back and stared at him in silence.

Master Dagg smirked. "Fear is not received well by many, is it? Your own fears are now melded within your very being."

"I fear you out of respect," Banin admitted. "It is something not easily earned from a Hemlock Hunter. You are a worthy opponent, Dragon. But this—this is *preposterous*!"

I managed to smile. Master Dagg had sacrificed himself and all that he knew and loved to prove a single point. In the end, he got what he wanted—and Banin got what he deserved.

Banin eventually dragged himself up and fled. The cave fell to an awkward silence.

Master Dagg took a moment to scan his laboratory, which was disheveled from recent use. He let out a deep, exhausted sigh and collapsed against the table.

I remained where I sat and continued watching the laboratory's entrance, in fear of Banin returning. But after several minutes, there was no further sign of the Hemlock Hunter.

"Master Dagg?" He still looked terrible. "Are you all right?"

He managed a weak smile. "I've never been better."

"You . . . you let him escape. Aren't you worried that he might return with reinforcements?"

He chuckled. "Hardly, my dear. He is no longer . . . a Dragon slayer. He is the very man they will consider a traitor and outcast to their cause. He will be the new prey . . . soon enough."

I began smiling at the thought, but it quickly faded when Master Dagg slumped further against the table.

"I cannot . . . maintain this body much longer," he murmured, looking at me with heavy-lidded eyes. "I've given you . . . the last part of me. Always keep it close to your heart. Protect it . . . with your life."

"With my life?" I blinked. "But I am dead, aren't I?"

He shook his head, and with shaking fingers, he held up the phylactery hanging around his own neck. I slowly cupped my hand around my own phylactery and felt its warmth. It contained pure magic, but it also felt as if something was actually living inside.

"Life preservation does not come . . . without a price," Master Dagg said. "I have sacrificed much . . . but I will be able to fulfill my desires and explore the many hidden treasures of the world." He gestured to the remainder of his beloved laboratory. "This, Jasmine . . . all this is yours. I've taught you the foundations of the art of death . . . and undeath. It is up to you to master it on your own, just as I have. . . ."

I got up from the examining table and approached him. "You sound as if I will never see you again."

He huffed in response.

I embraced his weak form, and rested my head upon his shoulder. "Master Dagg . . . are you leaving me?"

"I am leaving," he said, his voice shifting between a low growl and his human rasp, "to never return. Perhaps . . . in another life—or death—we will meet again."

He gasped and began shaking, as his body started to transform.

I held him tighter in a futile attempt to suppress the inevitable. "What . . . what is happening to you?"

"It is . . . my punishment for challenging the work of the gods. It is a curse of my own form . . . the result of many years as an arcanist. My life preserved. . . ."

I could no longer hold him as his skin hardened and his body grew larger, nearly encompassing the entire laboratory.

He let out a terrifying howl as he broke free of his tattered overcoat, and his body molded into the shape of a Dragon once more. The once beautiful, majestic ebony scales had rotted away to scraps of flesh. His age-yellowed bones poked through the scraps of skin. Much of his face was but a skull, where the scaly skin was torn and barely clung to the bone. Two green, glowing orbs had replaced his dragon eyes, and they pulsated with a magic unfamiliar to me. His wings were reduced to bony frames, the webbed membranes replaced by rotting pieces of torn, hanging flesh.

I gazed at him in awe. *How hauntingly beautiful he is.*

He shifted his weight until he stood on his grotesque, skeletal limbs. The walls crumbled, and several jars and books on shelves inadvertently got knocked to the ground by one of his wings.

"Master Dagg! Can you still hear me? Are you still a Dragon? Are you still alive?"

His green eyes stared at me intently.

I shivered. *Does he even remember who I am?*

"I am as much of a Dragon as I will ever be, Jasmine," he said, his tone ghastly but still recognizable. "I have shed my Draconic skin of the past in order to embrace the new unlife that awaits me. Ironically, I feel even more alive in this new body than I did in the last."

He turned and squeezed through the laboratory's entrance, rocks crumbling around the cavern's opening to accompany his large girth, and started for the cave entrance. Despite his frightful form, he walked with a normal gait like any other four-legged creature. His bony tail slithered along behind him, revealing that the last of his once-beautiful obsidian scales that hadn't yet crumbled away.

I watched him for a few moments before following.

Master Dagg stood in the midst of his beloved, death-ridden swamps and gazed at the sky. He stretched his bony wings to test the winds.

I rushed over to him and placed my hand over his tail. "Master Dagg! You can't possibly expect to—"

With a hiss and a quick whip of his tail, he shook off my touch. "Do not stop me. No one can stop me." Then he muttered, "No one but the gods."

I could no longer form the words to speak. The phylactery around my neck pulsated furiously, reflecting the pain of my heart. *He really is leaving me. . . .*

His green eyes flared as he looked at me. "Good-bye, Jasmine, and thank you."

He turned and leapt toward the evening's overcast sky. I had doubted his ability to fly, but the magical aura encompassing him apparently rendered it possible. The sounds of his wings flapping and of the air rushing through his skeletal form grew fainter as he drew further away.

I fell to my knees in the cold, murky water, my face still tilted toward the sky. Pleasant memories of Master Dagg's company flooded my mind, and I couldn't help but smile. He had truly helped me—and I, in turn, had helped him.

Perhaps I am not dead, after all. Perhaps this is only the beginning of a renewed life.

After Master Dagg's great form disappeared into the night sky, I clutched the phylactery, closed my eyes, and for the first time, felt a single tear roll down my cheek.

About the Author

R.M. PRIOLEAU is a game designer by day and dangerous writer by night. Since childhood, she's continued discovering new ways to expand her skills and creativity as she delves into the realm of literary abandon. When R.M. is not leveling up, RPing, or indulged in the latest old school fighting games and RPGs, she is hard at work advocating for great non-profit literacy movements and organizations. Find out more about the author at www.rmprioleau.com.